MARVEL

Spider-Man, Spider-Man!

MARVEL

Illustrations by Shane Clester
Designed by Scott Petrower

"Theme From Spider-Man"
Words and Music by J. Robert Harris and Paul Francis Webster
Performed by Kris Martin
Additional Vocals by Nick Peck and Billy Martin
Produced by Billy Martin
Published by Hillcrest Music and Webster Music ©1967/R1995 All rights reserved.
Lyrics Reprinted by Permission

Special Thanks to Gwen Riley

Printed in the United States of America

First Edition, October 2018   10 9 8 7 6 5 4 3

ISBN 978-1-368-02769-4

FAC-034274-19165

Library of Congress Control Number: 2018943180

Reinforced binding

Spider-Man, Spider-Man!

MARVEL

Los Angeles • New York

Spider-Man!

Does whatever a spider can!

Spins a web,
any size . . .

catches thieves
just like flies.

Here comes the **Spider-Man.**

Is he
strong?

Take a look overhead.

There goes the

THWIP!

Spider-Man.

In the chill
of night . . .

at the scene
of a crime . . .

Spider-Man,

Spider-Man!

Friendly neighborhood

Spider-Man!

Wealth and fame,
he's ignored.

ACTION
is
his
reward.

To him, life is a great big bang-up.

Wherever there's
a hang-up . . .

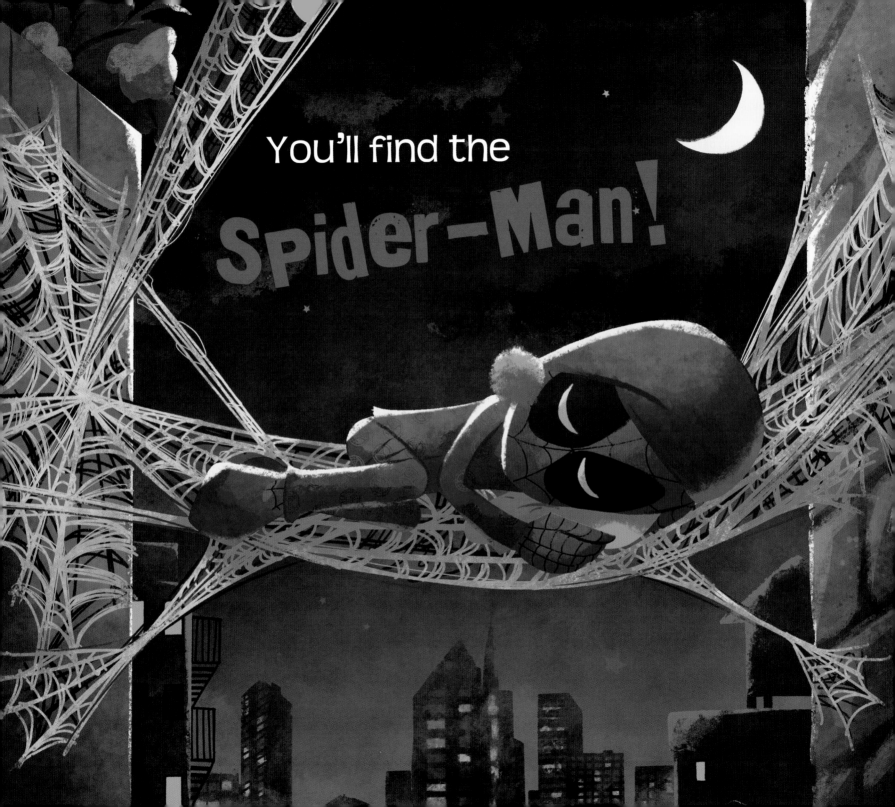

You'll find the

Spider-Man!